Frankie Wonders...
What Happened Today?

Written By

Yvonne Conte

Drawings by Anna Cerullo

Published by Amsterdam-Berwick Publishing Company

Frankie Wonders What Happened Today?

All of the net profits from the publication of this book will be donated to **The Children's Aid Society in New York City**. Since the events of September 11th, The Children's Aid Society has been providing emergency assistance for children and families in need at its centers and schools and at other city locations where help is needed. Starting the day of the attack, Children's Aid mobilized its medical and mental health staffs and provided counseling. They distributed medications, organized its caseworkers to help victims obtain assistance and helped train teachers to identify post-traumatic stress disorder and cope with children who may be depressed or anxious.

The Children's Aid Society is committed to help children lead healthy happy lives and become productive well-adjusted adults.

You can donate to the Children's Aid Society by calling 212-949-2936 or online at www.childrensaidsociety.org

Published by Amsterdam-Berwick Publishing Company.

Printed & Bound by Phoenix Graphics, Inc.

Typesetting by Golden Times.

Edited by Carla Jonquil.

Frankie Wonders...

What Happened Today?

Something strange was happening at Frankie's house. His sister Angela missed her ballet lesson and stayed in her leotards and tights all day long! There were a gazillion phone calls. His mommy even forgot to give him his vitamins!

Everyone was acting strange. Frankie's mommy cried all day. It scared him because as long as he could remember he had never seen his mommy cry. When his daddy came home from work that day, he hugged Frankie longer and harder than he ever had before. He acted like he hadn't seen him in a very long time. This was confusing because Frankie had seen his daddy that morning and everything seemed fine.

$\mathscr{F}$rankie knew something was not right. He was scared and confused. No one told him what was going on. Frankie was ANGRY! He was going to find out what happened today. Frankie stormed into the family room where everyone sat watching the news. "I want to know why this family is so sad!" Frankie demanded.

Frankie's daddy quickly turned the TV off and everything was quiet. His mommy got up from her chair and walked over to her son. "You are right, Frankie. We are very sad. Do you know what happened today?"

Frankie thought about what he had seen on TV and about what he heard his daddy talking about earlier. "I know that a big plane flew into a tall building," he said.

"Yes it did." Mommy nodded.

"And I know that it caught on fire and the whole building fell down! CRASH!" Frankie said with great expression.

"You are right. It did," said his dad. "We are all very sad right now because many people have been hurt and lost." Frankie seemed sad. "Were they your friends?"

"No. We didn't know any of the people who have been hurt," Frankie's mom explained. "It still makes us sad."

Frankie was quiet for a minute and then said, "Oh. That makes me very sad too."

Mommy hugged Frankie. "Is there anything else that you would like to talk about?"

Frankie thought of lots of questions. "Why did the plane crash into the building? Was it broken? Are more planes going to crash?"

"The plane wasn't broken," said Daddy. Frankie jumped up onto his daddy's lap to listen. "The plane didn't just fall out of the sky today. Some very bad people did this on purpose. They wanted to do something bad to Americans."

Frankie looked frightened. "Will they fly a plane into our house?"

"NO WAY!" Frankie's daddy assured him. "Our house is not a target."

"That's good," Frankie said, "because I like our house." Frankie believed his daddy. He knew his daddy was a very smart man.

"The buildings that were hit by planes, the World Trade Center and the Pentagon are very large buildings that symbolize the strength of our country. The bad people are angry with our country but they are not angry with you or me or mommy or Angela. We are safe and our home is safe. Does that make you feel any better?"

"Yep. But now I'm hungry! Is dinner ready yet?" asked Frankie. Frankie jumped down and ran into the kitchen.

*J*ust as Frankie was beginning to feel better, another strange thing happened. They had pancakes for dinner … and NO vegetable! "WOW! Pancakes for dinner! What a terrific surprise!" Frankie seemed like the only one who was happy about that. Everyone began to eat but no one talked. They all still seemed very sad. Were they afraid that the bad people were going to come after them too? Frankie didn't know but he wondered.

After dinner Angela helped her mommy with the dishes while Daddy read the paper. Frankie played quietly with his fire truck and wondered if their house would catch on fire like the building on TV.

Later he brushed his teeth and washed his face to get ready for bed. He put on his fireman pajamas and put his fire truck next to his bed. He even wore his bright red fireman's hat to bed! When his mommy came to tuck him in she laughed. "Are you going to sleep with your hat on?"

"Can I?" Frankie asked.

"Wouldn't it be a bit uncomfortable?" his mommy wondered.

"Well, if our house catches on fire, I'll be ready to save us."

"Oh," his mommy said. "You're worried that our house might catch on fire like the buildings on the TV did."

"Yep." Frankie looked worried.

Mommy thought for a minute. Then she gave Frankie a big hug and said, "I don't think we have anything to worry about."

Frankie wasn't convinced. "Are you sure?" he said.

Mommy and Frankie went into the hallway. "See this?" Mommy pointed to the ceiling just outside his door. "This is a fire alarm. If we did have a fire in here, a loud sound would wake us up and we could run outside to safety."

"Oh that's good," Frankie said with a sigh.

Back in Frankie's room, his mommy gave him a long hug and kissed him at the tip of his nose just as she had every night for as long as Frankie could remember. As she was about to leave, Frankie asked her, "Mommy, can I sleep with the light on tonight? Mr. Stuffy Bear is a little bit scared of the dark."

She smiled and said it was OK.

The next morning, Frankie picked up his spoon and began to eat his cereal. He looked up at his mommy and asked, "When Daddy dies will he go to Heaven?"

"Yes, he will go to Heaven, but he probably won't go for a very long time because Daddy is strong and healthy." She took a sip of her coffee and said, "We are all safe, Frankie, and we will all be ok." Frankie still looked a bit worried. All of a sudden his mommy began to smile and said, "I have a great idea."

Frankie looked up at his mommy. He was glad to see her look happy, and he wondered what her idea was.

"Let's go out to the garage and get our American flag and put it out front." She seemed so pleased to have thought of it.

Frankie's forehead wrinkled up as if he was thinking really hard. "Is it Flag Day?" he asked.

"No," answered his mommy.

"Well then," he thought for another minute, "Is it Memorial Day?"

Again she answered no. "I just want the world to know that we are proud Americans!"

*A*fter breakfast they went out to the garage to find the flag. There it was behind the extra lawn chairs in a big brown box with the red letters. Frankie carried it out to the front lawn and raised the flag.

"That sure is a big flag." He was a bit out of breath, and although didn't want to admit it, the flag was almost too big for him to carry.

"America is a good place to live, Frankie. It is a free country. Now we have to be extra careful to be sure we protect that freedom."

Frankie said, "I heard Daddy say we are at war. Are we fighting for our freedom?"

"Yes we are," said Mommy. She patted the top of Frankie's head. "You are such a smart little boy."

"Will Daddy have to fight the war?" Frankie asked.

"No, he is not a serviceman. But many good men and women are working very hard to protect us and keep us safe. Hundreds of rescue workers, firemen and policemen have gone to New York City to help people who have been hurt. Our President is working hard to find the bad people and keep us all safe."

Frankie thought for a minute. "Maybe I can take my fire truck and hat and help too?"

$\mathcal{F}$rankie's mommy smiled, "You know I think we can find something right here at home that we can do." She took out several sheets of drawing paper and lots of bright colored crayons, and together they began to draw delightful pictures to send to the firemen. Frankie worked all morning on his drawings. He drew wonderful yellow sunsets and beautiful tall trees, colorful flags and bright blue stars. He made mountains and valleys and busses and trains. All of Frankie's pictures were happy and full of joy.

"If the firemen start to feel sad, they can look at my pictures and feel happy again, right Mommy?"

"Right Frankie," she replied.

That afternoon they put all the drawings in a big yellow envelope and marked it **New York City Fire Fighters**. They walked to the post office and mailed it. Frankie felt very important because he had done something good to help the firefighters.

Several days passed and things seemed rather normal at Frankie's house. He played with his friends and watched his cartoons. Angela went to her ballet lessons and Frankie got his vitamin every morning. Mommy and Daddy read him lots of good stories before bed each night. In church that Sunday, the preacher talked about things Frankie didn't understand. People cried and everyone hugged more than usual. After church, Frankie and his family joined many people from the church and had a car wash to raise money for the American Red Cross. It was great fun. Everyone got very wet. They washed lots of cars and trucks and one big red fire truck! Frankie got to sit in the fire truck and ring the bell! He felt big and important, and it made him smile. The fire fighters gave everyone little American flags to keep. That was really neat.

That night when his mommy came to tuck him in, she noticed Frankie wasn't wearing his fireman's hat. "Frankie, I see you have decided it's not so comfortable with the hat on," she smiled.

"I don't have to wear my hat because I know the firemen will come and help us if we need them," he said.

"That's right!" his mommy said as she hugged him. "We love you very much. Everyone will do everything possible to keep us safe."

"I'm glad," said Frankie. "We sure did have fun today didn't we Mommy?"

"Yes we did. And we sure did get wet too!"

Frankie smiled. "We can still have fun even though some bad things have happened, right Mom?"

"Absolutely. In fact we should always try to find the good especially when bad things happen." She was quiet for a minute and then she said, "It was a wonderful thing the way we all came together today to raise money for the Red Cross. People all over our country are helping in many ways. Some are donating blood, others are raising money, and all of us are saying extra prayers too."

"Can we say a special prayer tonight?" asked Frankie.

"Sure we can. What would you like to pray about?"

Frankie closed his eyes and folded his hands and so did his mom. "Dear Lord, Thank you for Mommy and Daddy and Angela. Thank you for all my toys and for my fire truck. Please keep us safe and happy and help all the people who are hurt to feel better. Amen." With that his mommy kissed the tip of his nose. She turned out the light, and Frankie closed his eyes.

After she left the room, Frankie put his tiny hands together once again. "Excuse me, Dear Lord. But if you have a few more minutes I have something more to say. Please be sure to tell all our friends on the fire trucks that it's ok to feel happy about other things even if we are still sad in our hearts. Amen."

$\mathcal{F}$rankie was worried and then he was scared. He got very angry and then he was sad. He wished he could fix what happened but knew that he couldn't. However there are some things that we can do. Mommy and Frankie made a list. They want to share it with you and your mommy.

1. Make a pretty picture or nice letter to send to the workers.

2. Make cookies for the firefighters in your town to say thank you.

3. Hang a flag in your room!

4. Take extra time to hug and cuddle with the people you love.

5. Talk to your mom and dad when you feel scared or confused.

6. Tell your family about the things you are happy about or grateful for.

7. Volunteer at your church or school. It feels good to do something for someone else.

8. Have a garage sale or sell lemonade and donate the money you make to help others.

9. Remember that your mom and dad will always love you no matter what happens.

10. Say an extra prayer for the people hurt on September 11th.

We wish to thank the companies and individuals
who have reduced their fees to help us produce this book.

Phoenix Graphics, Inc. – Printing and Binding

Golden Times – Typesetting and much appreciated advice

Carla Jonquil – Editing

Anna Cerullo – Illustrations